Angels in Training

Story by Marsha Hammond

Art by Karen Dishaw

In the garden, goodness grows
angelic babes with bright halos.
They prepare and train to be
guardian angels watching thee.

Gloria Gail was blessed with heart,
angelic beauty and oh so smart.

Small Mae Ling was shy and sweet,
a perfect angel from head to feet.

Thoughtful Gabe was always thinking.
He's a worrier with halo blinking,
with the cutest freckles and bright red hair,
he longs to try things but does not dare.

While Faith was good and sweet and sharing,
she was also a bit too daring.
Her halo often slipped from place,
her white wings, too, in need of grace.

The sun was shining a butter yellow.
The skies were blue and oh so mellow.
The birds sang out their sweetest song.
Angelic Faith just skipped along.

Faith's world was turned all upside down.
She fell face first on sacred ground.

"Oh my stars! For heaven's sake!
How much bad luck can an angel take?"

Faith knew it wasn't luck at all,
just an untied shoelace that made her fall.

It seemed her friends did all things right.
With gowns all neat and halos bright.
How she wished to have been blessed
to be like them and neatly dressed.

She'd started out that very day
with golden hair, none gone astray.
Her wings were neat, her halo bright,
her angel gown a perfect white.
She'd made a plan to stay that way.
She'd sit real still while others play.

In the garden beside the gate,
Faith and friends must sit and wait
for Mrs. Flyright to return
with flight instructions for them to learn.

When breezes flow through angel hair
and rainbows fill the sky and air,
when slides of many shades and hues
call, "Play with us!" Faith can't refuse.

Before Faith knew, she'd flown up high
And played on rainbows in the sky.

Her little wings were not too strong.
They could fly but not too long.
Cautious Gabe, back on the ground,
called, "Little friend, please do come down!"

The angel jumped from cloud to cloud.
Gabe closed his eyes, "That's not allowed!"
She climbed aboard a rainbow ride
where angel friends could slip and slide.

She slipped and slid and laughed out loud.
She slid right off and caught a cloud.
Gabe began to wish he, too,
could put this on his list to do.

Faith waved at Gabe on tippy toe.
Then all at once strong winds did blow.
Unafraid, Faith only wiggled,
pushed back her halo and simply giggled.

Her friends called out down on the ground,
"Forgetful you! You must come down!"

Her friends were right. Now she must go
to flying class way down below.
With goodbye kisses from angel lips,
she waved goodbye and turned and tripped...

Faith's good friends were wondering why
Mrs. Flyright had not come by.
And what of Faith, their daring friend?
Where could she be? Where had she been?

They did not see her hiding there
with skinned up knee and tangled hair.
They did not know where she had been
before she tumble-bumbled in.

Faith began to think things through.
She remembered rules and lists to do,
and how her wings, now torn and bent,
had been a gift and heaven sent.
She thought of halos and gowns of white.
And prayed someday to make things right.

Mae Ling ran around a giant tree,
"Oh me oh my, friends, look and see!"
Gabe looked high up inside the tree.
"Oh, angel wings! How could it be?"

There was Faith, right where she landed.
Took out a bird's nest single-handed.
The view was all she ever hoped,
but coming down a slippery slope.

Her wings got caught on branches long.
She pulled them loose. It all went wrong.
It seemed she freed her grasp instead
and fell into the flower bed.

Daisies peaked through angel hair.
Her halo bent and held them there.
Faith's little friends brought her rescue,
but such a mess they never knew.

One tried to straighten both her wings.
Another worked on grass-stained things.
Her gown was torn, a big disgrace.
Her hair streamed down her angel face.

Gloria tried to straighten wings,
but they were crumpled, messy things.
They hoped their teacher would never know
of Faith's descent to grounds below.

Mrs. Flyright shouted, "Form a line.
It's angel inspection number nine."
She found her students quite undone.
Especially that messy one.

The teacher questioned as to why
Faith's halo fell across one eye,
but when she spread her crooked wing,
her teacher then knew everything.

She picked a daisy from Faith's hair
and tapped her foot, just standing there.
"Class dismissed," the teacher said.
That's when she saw the flower bed.
A row of daisies, all but gone
just like the ones that Faith had on.

"A rainbow waved across the sky.
My wings waved back, and so did I,
and at its end, a rainbow slide,
whose colors called to come and ride.
I answered yes, so up I went.
I fell and now my wings are bent."

"I'm oh so sorry and feel so bad.
I should have listened. I wish I had."

With that, she curtsied her head bowed down.
Her halo slipped, fell on the ground.
It clinked and clanged, an awful sound.
It blinked and spun 'round and 'round.
It wibble-wobbled on the ground,
and then it made a buzzing sound.

She hit the ground with both her knees,
grabbed her halo quick as you please.
She clutched it tightly to her chest.
She closed her eyes and did her best
to disappear from where she knelt.
Can you imagine how she felt?

Faith counted to ten and held her breath.
She closed one eye, still scared to death.
But everything was still the same.
She heard her teacher call her name.

"Keep the faith, my little friend.
Now open your eyes and start again."

This little angel who began her day
neat and tidy had gone astray.
Instead she now was one hot mess.
Her halo blinked an S.O.S.

Much to Faith's immense surprise,
Her teacher looked deep in her eyes.
She even looked into her soul.
Then said, "Now, Faith, you take control."

"For just like you, all go astray.
God knew that man would be that way.
And angels, too, must sometimes seek
strength and wisdom to help the weak."

"Dear Faith, you're lucky you're not hurt.
Just a crooked wing and a smudge of dirt.
Now fix your hair up off your face.
And thank the Lord for His good grace."

Just like Faith, we sometimes, too,
have done some things we should not do.
And afterward, it hurts to know
that we've been where we should not go.

So what to do when we know we're wrong,
when our conscience hurts us all day long?
An understanding God have we.
Forgiveness is the golden key.

He made the angels and rainbows, too.
God made me, and He made you.
He guides us all to do what's right.
He sends us love both day and night.
All He asks us in return
is to love Him first and try to learn,
to love our neighbors as ourselves
'cause that's the greatest kind of wealth.

So remember children now listen here.
You need not worry. You need not fear.
Just follow all the golden rules.
Live what you learn, in church and school.

And don't forget this lesson too.
When you fail, God still loves you.
He only wants you to do your best.
So keep Him first. He'll do the rest.

Little angels, too young to fly
are turning cartwheels in the sky.
Tiny tots on streets of gold
await the day their wings unfold.
An artful rainbow fills the sky.
Colors form a promise high.
A promise made, a promise kept
to save mankind while storm clouds wept.
God made a rainbow of many hues,
pinks and purples, violet blues.
Heaven's children, a rainbow ride,
angel friends who slip and slide.
Hear them laugh with pure delight,
playful friends with halos bright,
who practice how to use their wings,
those feathered, temperamental things.
They sometimes fall instead of soar,
but they just stand and try once more.
They don't stop to cry and mope
for angel wings are filled with hope.
Clouds that float of fluffy white,
marshmallow sweet, a saint's delight,
a place to rest on gentle breeze
pillow soft, above the trees.
Heaven's tots get sleepy too,
but Jesus knows just what to do.
He picks them up with nail-pierced hands.
He holds them close, He understands.
He wraps them gently in angel wings,
soft lullabies they sweetly sing.
God's guardian angels are taught to fly,
unseen protection in the sky.
From soaring spirit to earthly shield.
protective hand of God revealed.

DEDICATED TO MY INFANT GRANDDAUGHTER, AVERY,
WHO PLAYS AMONG THE ANGELS.